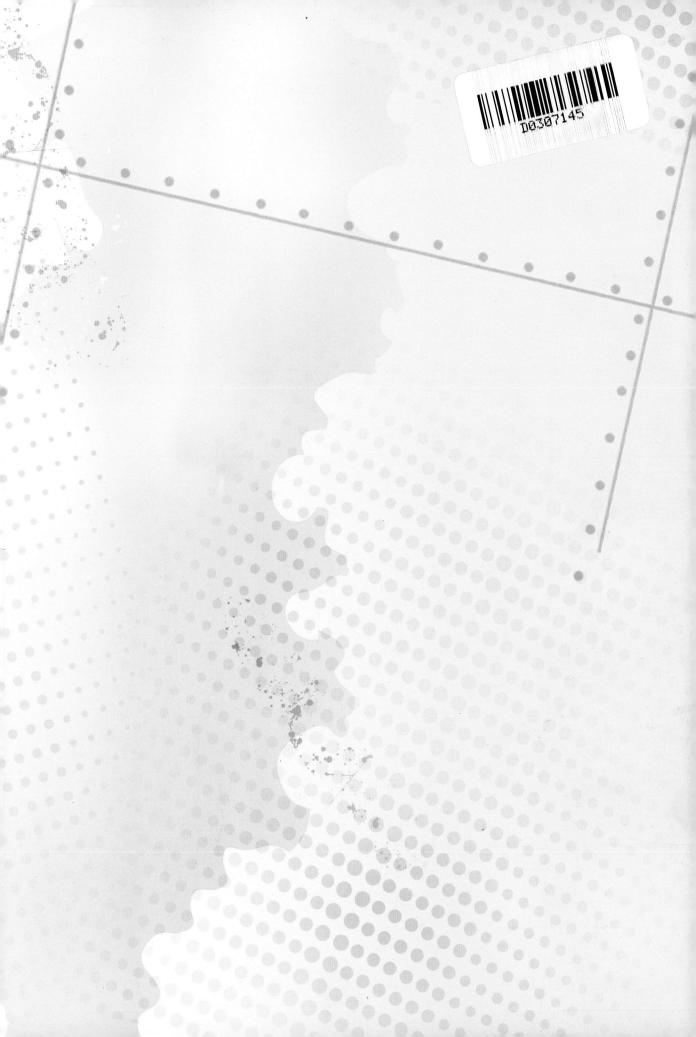

D0307145

First published by Parragon in 2013

Parragon
Chartist House
15–17 Trim Street
Bath BA1 1HA, UK
www.parragon.com

Adapted by Ellie O'Ryan
Illustrated by the Disney Storybook Artists

ISBN 978-1-4454-9677-1

Printed in China

Bath · New York · Singapore · Hong Kong · Cologne · Delhi
Melbourne · Amsterdam · Johannesburg · Shenzhen

Dusty is a small-town crop-dusting plane with a big dream. He wants to race in the Wings Around The Globe Rally with the fastest planes in the world. He loves racing so much he even daydreams about it – especially when he is working!

Dusty's best friend is a fuel truck called Chug. He gives Dusty racing instructions over a radio to help Dusty practise for the rally. Eventually, though, Chug decides Dusty needs someone who knows more about flying to train him.

Dusty visits Dottie, the local mechanic, to be repaired. She realizes that she has been fixing him a lot recently. Dottie asks Dusty if he has been racing.

Dusty lies and says he hasn't been racing, but Chug blurts out the truth.

"You're not built to race," Dottie tells Dusty. She is afraid that he is going to crash if he keeps it up.

Chug takes Dusty to see Skipper, a grumpy old warplane, to see if he can help Dusty. Skipper used to be in the Jolly Wrenches, a navy squadron, and is known as a wartime hero.

"Go home. You're in over your head, kid," says Skipper.

Dusty leaves, sad and disappointed.

Chug carries on training Dusty and soon it is time for the Wings Around The Globe Rally qualifying race.

At the airstrip a three-times rally winner called Ripslinger makes a big entrance. His teammates, Ned and Zed, make sure everyone notices him.

"He's so good, he doesn't need to qualify – he's already in the rally!" Dusty exclaims.

Finally, it is Dusty's turn for his qualifying lap. As he rolls towards the starting line, Ripslinger makes fun of him for being a 'racing' crop duster. The crowd start to laugh at him!

Dusty tries to focus as he prepares for take-off.
He needs to finish in fifth place to qualify.
Everyone watches in amazement as Dusty has an impressive run!

Dusty speeds over the finish line and Dottie and Chug rush over to congratulate him. They are so proud of their friend for not giving up!

But when the results come up, Dusty has only finished in sixth place – he has not qualified for the rally!

Dusty is so upset that he decides to give up racing.

Then one afternoon, a race official comes to Propwash Junction with some news. Another racer has been disqualified, which means Dusty is going to the Wings Around The Globe Rally after all!

Skipper finally agrees to train Dusty. He pushes his student to fly higher because the tailwind above the clouds will give Dusty more speed. But Dusty keeps making excuses for why he can't fly higher.

"The Jolly Wrenches have a motto: *Volo Pro Veritas*. It means 'I fly for truth', which clearly you don't!" Skipper scolds.

Poor Dusty has to admit he is keeping a secret: he is afraid of heights!

Skipper has an idea. He has Dusty race the shadow of a passenger plane that flies over Propwash Junction every day.

That way, Dusty can practise racing without flying too high.

Dusty works hard. Soon Skipper tells him he is ready for the rally.

Dusty flies to New York to join the other racers for the start of the event.

He meets a racer from England called Bulldog. The famous flyer isn't very friendly. "This is a competition," Bulldog tells Dusty. "Every plane for himself."

Dusty wants to meet all of the planes, but he is shy and doesn't know what to say to them.

Suddenly, a masked plane makes an exciting entrance as he flies into pit row. No one recognizes him, except Dusty.

"It's El Chupacabra! He's the indoor racing champion of Mexico!" explains Dusty. El Chu is also a singer and a TV star.

El Chu and Dusty become instant friends.

The Wings Around The Globe Rally has several stages. During the first stage the racers have to fly over the Atlantic Ocean. Dusty flies right through the middle of a freezing hailstorm. He can hardly see and almost crashes into an iceberg!

The next stage of the rally is a night flight to Germany. On the way Bulldog gets into serious trouble. Leaking oil covers his windscreen and he can't see where he is going. Dusty springs into action!

Dusty flies alongside the English racer, telling him where to fly, and helps him land safely. Bulldog is surprised to see it is Dusty who helped him, especially since it means that Dusty is now in last place.

In Germany Dusty meets Franz, a little car who can turn into a plane called Von Fliegenhosen.

Franz asks Dusty, "Wouldn't you fly faster without the tank and pipes weighing you down?"

Dusty removes his crop-dusting gear and flies around with El Chu and Von Fliegenhosen. What a great idea! He feels like a new plane!

Being lighter, Dusty flies like a new plane, too! In the third stage of the rally he passes one racer after another, weaving through the mountains in India. Flying low round obstacles is Dusty's speciality!

Dusty moves from last place all the way up to eighth place. It is all anyone can talk about! Ripslinger, who is known as the Green Tornado, is angry at all the attention Dusty is getting. He is supposed to be the star of the rally!

Back in Propwash Junction, Skipper watches Dusty being interviewed on TV. Suddenly, he feels inspired!

Skipper's friend Sparky pushes him on to the runway in Propwash Junction. Skipper takes a deep breath and starts his engine.

But he can't do it – he can't bring himself to fly.

Back at the rally, the race to Nepal has begun.
The other racers head over the mountains.

Dusty has been told that he can follow the train tracks
through the valley, instead of flying high. As Dusty follows
the tracks he sees that they disappear into a tunnel.

Dusty tries to face his fear so that he can fly high over the mountain, but he can't do it so he has to fly through the tunnel!

He makes it out of the other side just in time – a train is coming!

Dusty reaches Nepal and lands in a quiet valley. "Have the other racers left already?" Dusty asks an official.

"No, no one else is here yet," he replies. "You're in first place!"

Dusty has become the star of the rally! He has millions of fans from all over the world. They cheer him on as he flies the next stage to Shanghai in China.

Dusty is now Ripslinger's main competition. Dusty is the biggest story on the news, which makes Ripslinger very angry.

While he is in China Dusty talks to his friends back home about the next stage of the rally.

He has to fly across the Pacific Ocean to Hawaii and then on to Mexico.

"There will be monsoons," warns Skipper. "They can tear your wings right off. Be careful."

Chug announces that he has a surprise – the Propwash gang is going to meet Dusty in Mexico!

As the racers fly over the Pacific Ocean one of Ripslinger's sidekicks sneaks up on Dusty and breaks off his antenna. Dusty is lost without it!

Dusty tries to find somewhere to land but he is quickly running out of fuel!

Suddenly, two navy fighter jets pull up beside him. They tell him to follow them to their aircraft carrier.

On board the aircraft carrier Dusty finds photos of Skipper on the Jolly Wrenches' Wall of Fame. Bravo and Echo, the two jets that helped him, are also in the Jolly Wrenches.

Dusty sees that Skipper is only on the list for one mission. Skipper admits over the radio that he only flew once and never flew again – he is no war hero.

There is a storm approaching so Dusty has to quickly refuel, be fixed with a new antenna and set off to finish the race.

Dusty is catapulted off the aircraft carrier
for take-off, just like the navy planes. He is
on his way to Mexico!

As Dusty flies over the Pacific Ocean rain pours down and lightning flashes around him. He is flying so low that he gets caught in a wave. He makes a desperate call for help before he is swept underwater.

A Mexican Navy helicopter arrives just in time to rescue him.

After being rescued, Dusty is taken to the hangar in Mexico where his friends are waiting for him.

Dusty asks Skipper why he lied about the missions he had flown.

Skipper tells Dusty that he lost his whole squadron on the mission. After that, he was too afraid to fly again.

Dusty is sad and angry that Skipper lied to him. To make matters worse, he is too damaged to fly in the next stage of the rally.

However, the other racers, including his new friends Bulldog and El Chu, decide to help Dusty and give him their spare parts. Now he can be repaired and finish the rally!

Dusty is supercharged and heading to New York in the last stage of the rally. He is determined to win! Ripslinger, however, has other plans.

"Let's end this," Ripslinger calls to Ned and Zed as he tries to knock Dusty out of the race.

Suddenly, Skipper comes roaring into view and saves Dusty. Dusty can't believe Skipper is flying again!

"Go get 'em!" Skipper calls to Dusty as Ripslinger zooms off towards New York.

Dusty knows there is only one way to catch up with Ripslinger: to fly high above the clouds and use a tailwind for speed. He finally faces his fear – and punches through the clouds!

Dusty whoops with excitement as he rockets forward.
Soon he catches sight of New York — and Ripslinger,
who is flying below him.

When they reach the finish line, Dusty swerves past Ripslinger, who is posing for the cameras, and wins!

Dusty's pals are so proud of him and he is grateful for their help. But Dusty's biggest thanks goes to Skipper. He helped Dusty to victory and is still his hero, no matter what!

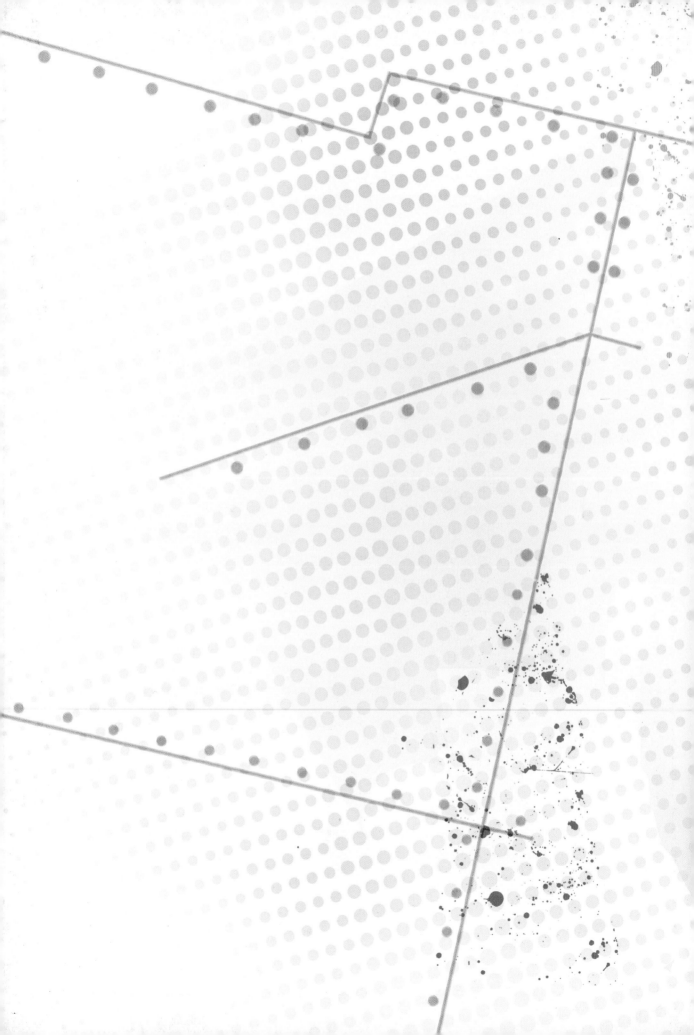